Giant lobsters freed

Any crustacean old enough to weigh 25 pounds is entitled to end where she began: in the depths of the deep blue sea. That's how the State of Maine sees it.

Shirley, the 25-pounder, and her companion, Bob, who weighs nearly 20 pounds, have frolicked in the Maine waters for a long time. Had they been caught by a local lobsterman, they'd have been returned to the sea at once because Maine law protects crustaceans with body shells longer than five inches. Unfortunately, however, Shirley and Bob were snagged in a dragger's net and brought to Rhode Island....

From *The New York Times*

For my mother, Sylvia Margolin

Bob and Shirley: A Tale of Two Lobsters
Text copyright © 1991 by Harriet Ziefert
Illustrations copyright © 1991 by Mavis Smith
Printed in Singapore. All rights reserved.
Produced by Harriet Ziefert, Inc.
ISBN 0-06-107427-6 (pbk.)
First Paperback Edition, 1991
News article on page one copyright © 1988
by The New York Times Company. Reprinted by permission.

Library of Congress Cataloging-in-Publication Data
Ziefert, Harriet.
    Bob and Shirley : a tale of two lobsters / by Harriet Ziefert ;
pictures by Mavis Smith. — 1st ed.
        p.   cm. — (An amazing animal reader!)
    Summary: Two old lobsters are caught and put in a tank in a fish
store window until some concerned humans picket the store.
    ISBN 0-06-026908-1 (lib. bdg.). — ISBN 0-06-107427-6 (pbk.)
    [1. Lobsters—Fiction.] I. Smith, Mavis, ill. II. Title.
III. Series.
PZ7.Z487Bo   1991
[E]—dc20

90-43150
CIP
AC

An Amazing Animal Reader!

BOB AND SHIRLEY

A TALE OF TWO LOBSTERS

by Harriet Ziefert • pictures by Mavis Smith

HarperCollins*Publishers*

Bob and Shirley were lobster friends.
Shirley was at least forty years old.
She might even have been a hundred!
Bob was younger than Shirley.
How much younger, no one knew.

Bob and Shirley lived a quiet life.
Their home was in the cool waters
near Maine.

They crawled along the ocean floor,
often side by side.

One foggy day Bob and Shirley were caught in a huge net. They were carried off to Rhode Island.

There they were dumped onto a dock.
A dock worker put bands around their big claws.

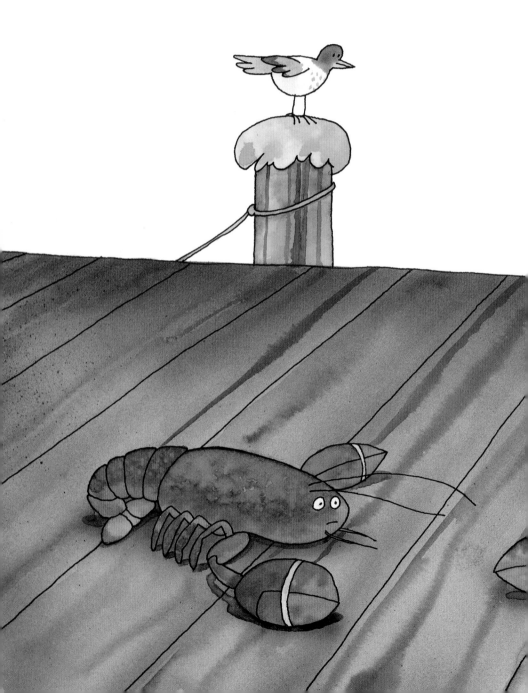

Then Bob and Shirley were sold
to a Long Island seafood dealer.

Soon they were packed with ice, seaweed, and newspapers. They were trucked to New York.

Bob and Shirley spent the night in a crate.

The next morning they were packed again.
They were taken to a Philadelphia fish market.

The fish store owner proudly placed Bob
and Shirley in a 250-gallon tank in his window.

Lots of people came to look at the two giant
lobsters from Maine.

A carpenter saw the two lobsters
on his way home from work.
"How much?" he asked.

The store owner answered, "For Bob—$128. For Shirley—$160. If you take them both, I'll make it an even $270."

"It's a deal!" said the carpenter. "Here's some of the money. I'll be back on Friday."

By the end of the week, a number of people heard about Bob and Shirley.
They stood outside the fish market with signs.

NO SALE!

SAVE THE LOBSTERS NOW!

SAVE BOB

VE

LEY!

The owner did not like the angry people
outside his shop. He called the carpenter.
The carpenter agreed to buy eight,
six-pound lobsters, instead of Bob and Shirley.

So Bob and Shirley were again packed in crates with ice, seaweed, and newspapers.

They were put on an airplane.
They were flown back to Maine.

At the airport they were loaded onto a truck.
They were driven to the dock.

A lobsterman picked Bob up by his claws and tail. He gently lifted Bob over the side of his boat.

Another lobsterman gently lifted Shirley onto the same boat.

The lobsterman pulled away from the dock and headed toward the open sea.

After a half hour ride, he cut his engines.
He clipped the bands from Bob's claws, then
threw him off the side of the boat.
"If he's a Maine lobster," the man said, "this
is where he belongs."

Then the man returned Shirley to the sea.
Now Bob and Shirley were free to swim side
by side in cool waters—perhaps for another 40 years.

Amazing!

Amazing Animal Activities

1. Find an amazing story about two animal friends in a magazine or newspaper. Ask a librarian or other grown-up for help, if you need it.

2. Tell or write an amazing story about animal friends you know. Or make one up! If you like, draw pictures and make your own storybook.

3. Lobsters belong to a group of creatures called *crustaceans*. Look up crustaceans in an encyclopedia. Are you surprised to find what other animals are related to lobsters? What do they all have in common?

4. Have a grown-up take you on a trip to a fish market, aquarium, or some other place where you can see lobsters up close. Tell or write what you think it would be like to be a lobster.